A Very Kurious Anthology

**Kurious
Press**

Published by Kurious Press 2020

The moral rights of the authors have been asserted

www.kurious.art

ISBN: 978-1-9163622-1-5

Oh hello.

Welcome to the first *Very Kurious Anthology*. We're extremely pleased to see you.

As the veritable new kids on the block, we thought we'd kick off with a little bit of background about who we are, what we do & why we do it:

Kurious Arts is an arts incubation, events and production company, on a mission to support and showcase pioneering creativity in the North. Our focus is on capturing, curating and showcasing a range of multi-disciplinary creative activities via producing film, poetry, music, documentary, podcasts, live performance and now—an anthology of wonderfully curious short stories.

We also support the development of creative talent through an eclectic live-events programme, plus masterclasses, networking opportunities and of course—competitions.

We launched this, our first story competition, in October 2019, when one of our original members, David Oakley, suggested it and we said 'yes'. Saying 'yes' is our favourite thing to do, particularly in response to one of our members. Rejection, negativity and the word 'no' tend to feature highly in creative industries—it's just the nature of the beast, which is why we strive to do the opposite. We aim to bellow 'yes' to new ideas, 'yes' to collaboration, 'yes' to blue-sky-out-of-the-box-off-the-wall thinking. If we don't know how to make something happen, we work it out.

We were thrilled to receive over 137 entries

nationwide and had a very hard time whittling it down to the ten shortlisted stories you're about to read (eleven if you include the exclusive 'bonus' story generously contributed by Julianne Pachico, one of our judges). Our intention was to select a diverse collection based on the theme 'curious' to showcase the literary talent across the city and beyond. The final ten were sent to our three esteemed judges: Emma Bolland, Julianne Pachico and Niki Chang. One glance at their biogs at the back of this anthology serves to establish their striking credentials. After ranking all the stories, we ended up with joint winners, and each judge selected an additional 'highly commended' story.

Over the following pages you'll be whisked from the streets of São Paulo, to a hidden city in the treetops, from remote, rural Ireland to a post-apocalyptic world where Marmalade is gold-dust, and back home to the deeply ambiguous contents of a domestic refrigerator. Fingers crossed you've packed your passport.

We hope you enjoy these stories as much as we did. And if you're curious about Kurious, pop into Castle House for a cup of tea/coffee/wine & a chat. Or head to our weird website.

Letty Butler
Creative Director, Kurious Arts
www.kurious.art

PS. Watch out for next year's competition. Low entry fee, big prize, strong judges. What's not to like?

A note on the selection process by Emma Bolland

The entries fell roughly into two groups: those that positioned the short story as having a beginning, middle, and end, in which the end contains a kind of 'ta-da!' reveal, a 'I didn't see that coming' neat conclusion, or twist that stitches up and encloses, and those that treated the short story form as a more exploratory space, in which something is set out, observed, presented, that offers space for the reader to breathe. Of course, my opinions and preferences are subjective (as will be those of any judge) but I feel that the latter group, those that gave the reader space and agency, were the stronger. My 'top six', to varying degrees, fell into this category of 'openness', and as such were less easily discarded after reading, less used up: they continued to live in that they generated thinking beyond the page.

The joint winners were: *Land of Cardboard*, and *The Gestation Period of a Lemon*.

The 'highly commended' awards were given by the judges as follows:

Emma Bolland—*Grounding*
Julianne Pachico—*A Bell, A Step, A Cry*
Niki Chang—*A Healer's Touch*.

Contents

Marmalade

The marmalade glows like the ceiling lights. It's orange, like tinned carrots, but not as solid. You can look through it and see the rubbish pile. The tins are stretched and squashed, their neat rows wobbly-waving.

Mum breaks the seal and lets me smell. It's super-sweet, sickly sweet. Inside my nose it's warm and sharp and too much.

She spreads the marmalade onto crackers, careful not to waste a drop. The knife clatters in the tiny glass jar. My poorly tooth throbs.

Smiling, she puts the plate on my bed. 'Happy hundred-day.'

I count the tally marks on the wall. Twenty sets of five in the bottom row. The days have dragged on forever. We've run out of paper, so I can't even draw.

I'm scared to eat. Yesterday, I bit a dried pea too hard and my tooth broke. Mum rubbed her forehead and groaned when I cried. Since then I've tried not to whine.

I take the teeniest tiniest bite. Pain slices my tooth, all bright-bright ouchy and impossible to ignore.

The marmalade sparkles, teasing me. I like other foods: tinned carrots, oat mush, meat paste on crackers. Sometimes I count the hours until lunch or dinner. But nothing tastes like marmalade. Mum only lets me have it on hundred-days.

'Is it good?' she asks, licking her lips.

I tell her it's yum-yum-yum and do my biggest smile so that she won't cry or shout.

Mum takes a dry cracker for herself. I wish I could give her the marmalade, but I know she wouldn't take it. Her bones press through her cheeks like they want to break out. Lately she moves slower and slower. Her hands are always cold.

'Mum,' I say. 'Where does marmalade come from?'

'From the jar.'

'How did the jar get here?'

Mum sighs. She doesn't like it when I ask too many questions.

'Now, Alice,' she says. 'We've been through this.'

'The jars come from God.'

'That's right.'

'Where did God come from?'

'Alice,' Mum says. 'That's enough.'

When she turns to put away the jar, I slip off my sock, put the goopy crackers inside, and push it under my pillow.

Mum looks surprised to see my plate empty. I rub my tummy and do a big yawn.

'Right,' she says. 'Bedtime.'

I clean my teeth, keeping the brush away from the hurty side of my mouth. We used to use white paste that tasted cold and made bubbles, but we ran out. I asked Mum if more would come, like how the water tank fills back up if you wait long enough for the drip-drip-drips to collect. She said no. Only water works like that.

I grin to show her: all clean. She looks pleased as I climb into bed.

On a normal hundred-day, I sleep as soon as I've finished the marmalade, slip-sliding into sweet, tangy dreams. Tonight, I'm still awake when Mum finishes our bedtime prayer. Her eyelids keep flopping down over her lovely blue eyes.

'When will God give us more marmalade?' I ask.

'Soon, hopefully,' she says. 'Now get some sleep.'

Even after she turns off the ceiling lights, leaving just the dim green ones along the bottom of the walls, I'm wide awake.

When she gets out of bed, I think maybe she's going to the toilet. But she goes away from the curtain that hides the toilet and stumbles over to where the dress-up suit is hanging.

The suit is orange. Solid carrot-orange, not glowy orange like marmalade. Mum puts it on when she wants me to laugh. It's plasticy, like a packet of dried peas, not soft like clothes, so it makes a crinkle-crinkle noise when she moves. There's a hood with a funny face that zips over Mum's head with two big black eyes and a round mouth like she's shocked. The mouth sticks out like a tin.

I've tried putting on the suit, but it's too heavy for me. Mum said there is metal in the lining but she doesn't know why.

She struggles to get her arms in. I want to help, but whenever I wake up at night, she tells me I have to sleep and groans like I'm a big problem, and I hate that. So, I lie still and watch while she puts the suit on. Maybe she knows I'm sad and wants to surprise me.

But Mum doesn't come to my bed. Instead she picks up the click-click tube. I call it that because it's always making clicking noises. It has a mind of its own; there won't be a click for ages and then it'll do two or three one after the other. I've asked Mum what it's for, but she says: 'I don't know', 'have faith' or, lately, 'don't touch that.'

A light comes on. Not the big lights in the ceiling, or the dim green floor lights, but a tiny light she holds in her hand. She points it at the bit of the wall that's made of metal, all ridges and bumps that are nice to run your hands over when you're bored.

I'm often bored. Sometimes I spend an hour just standing on one leg, trying not to fall over, and then swap. So far my record is four fall-overs on the left leg and seven on the right.

Mum reaches up to the top, where there are some grey bumps I can't reach, and pokes at them. The suit covers her hands so her finger is stumpy like a carrot.

At first I think my eyes are wrong. Maybe it only looks like the ridgey wall slides away and leaves a hole. But then Mum steps into it and disappears.

I sit up in bed, fixing my eyes on the hole. Surely soon they must stop being confused and bring back Mum. But they don't. I can hear the suit going rustle rustle-rustle like she's moving, so maybe she's still there, inside the wall.

I wiggle out of bed. My feet tangle in the sheets, so I go thump on the floor. I think Mum might hear, but then I remember you can hardly hear anything with the suit-hood pulled up. I untangle myself from the sheets and go over to the hole in the wall, all careful-quiet, scared it might eat me too.

The wall closes like a mouth biting shut. I jump back as the metal slides into place, cutting me off from Mum. I try to pull it open, but it won't budge. I want to shout, but my tooth is hurting more than ever and my voice comes out as a whimper.

Now I'm angry. The wall won't give Mum back. I drag one of the chairs—the good one that's never been broken—away from the table and press it up against the wall. I climb onto the chair and press the bumps in the pattern Mum did, right before she disappeared.

The hole opens up again.

The air feels all funny. It moves like Mum's breath on my face when she hugs me, but cold. A monster's breath. I want to get back in bed and hide under the duvet, but Mum might be in danger, so I take a deep breath of my own and step into the dark.

She's disappeared. I scrunch up my face and rush forward on my tippy toes to keep away from the cold floor. One step it's a normal smooth, hard floor; the next, it's all lumpy and slimy. I almost fall down, but all those hours I've practiced standing on one leg pay off. I keep my balance as I run forward, my toes slip-sliding over the bumps.

I'm concentrating so hard on not falling down that at first I don't notice the blackness up ahead is now dark blue-grey. It's my eyes, I think, but I keep going and soon see that the hole I'm in opens up.

There's a whooshing noise. A bit like Mum snoring, a steady rhythm that comforts me in the dark.

The opening ahead isn't a rectangle like the hole I came in through. It's more like an open mouth with wonky teeth. I just want to get out of the dark, so I keep going, shivering in my jim-jams, through the mouth, towards the whoosh. The teeth don't bite me. I finally stumble out into … what is *this?*

The ceiling is so high I can't tell where it is. There's a round white light above, dim enough that I can stare at it without my eyes hurting but bright enough to light up everything. It's covered in little circles and there's a bit missing from the side, like it's a cracker and someone has taken a bite.

The ground under my feet goes all soft and powdery. It feels nice to wiggle my toes into.

In front is a big water, more water than I've ever seen. It would fill our tank a hundred million billion times, and it's all just spilled on the ground. It's going in and out, in and out, but I can't see what's moving it.

This is bad. You mustn't spill water. It takes a long time for the tank to refill. Mum would be mad.

Mum.

Why didn't she tell me all this was here, behind the wall? The moving water grabs the light and shines it back, all broken up. The big round light above is more beautiful than any of our lights at home. Somehow, it feels more real.

There's a rattling noise, like dried peas the time I spilled them on the floor. I turn to my left and see Mum walking along the edge of the water, holding the click-click tube, and I realise that's what's making the noise. The clicks are coming so fast it sounds like growling.

I'm suddenly scared. If she knows I followed her out, she'll be shouty or, worse, start to cry. I dive back into the dark and run all the way home.

I throw myself into bed and pretend to be asleep. My feet are damp but also feel hot. They're tingly and they hurt, not as bad as my tooth, but nearly.

A few minutes later, I hear noises behind the wall. Rustling. Water rushing. And then it stops and Mum reappears. She looks tired as she peels off the wet suit. The click-click tube has calmed down again, clicking only now and again as Mum sits on her bed with her head in her hands. Is she crying?

I want to comfort her, but she doesn't like me to see her cry. After ages and ages she gets into bed.

I'm too excited to sleep. My tummy flip-flops, and I think I might be sick. Under my pillow, I touch the sock I hid there. Perhaps if I don't eat the marmalade, next time, I can stay awake again and follow Mum out. Or maybe if I talk her into bringing me along, we can look around the big place together. Or maybe I'll wait until she's asleep, climb up on a chair, and press the grey bumps until the hole opens for me. My toes wiggle at the thought of running into the water, letting the silvery light shine on my skin.

A Healer's Touch

We are waiting for him.

His knocks are as gentle as a patter of rain, and one of us, Finula, the young one with hair bright as morning, opens the door to him. He looks holy, wind beaten and unshaven, like the Son of God Himself. He is dressed in an oilskin, and in the gap where it falls open, we can just make out a jumper, thick wool trousers and, on his feet, large leather boots. He flashes his teeth when he sees the round, young shape of our Finula. Collectively we draw in our breaths and try not to look afraid.

Behind him, the wind bends our hawthorn tree, flapping the clooties, the fabric strips we tied to the branches to scare away strangers like him who happen to be on the road.

'Could I bother you for a drink of water?' are the first words out of him.

You'd be most welcome to some, we say. *We have a well just out by that tree with the sweetest tasting water in all of Ireland.*

Siobhan and Maebh fall over themselves to get him a glass—it's been a while since we've had a man in the house. Our bodies thrill with that feeling of excitement and fear that men bring. Old Roisin offers him a seat by the fire. He lowers himself into it, smiling his sharp teeth at us, nodding at us in turn. His oilskin drips rainwater onto the floor. The table is scrubbed clean, ready.

'Just you ladies here today, then?' he says, probing, curious.

We all nod and say, *Oh yes, Sure, aren't the men still in the fields?*

'I didn't see anyone on my way over.' He's placing the glass of water on the floor. He looks up at Roisin. 'Not a soul for days,' he says.

You poor man, we say. *Isn't it lucky you came to us, then? Our husbands must've been digging inside holes too low in the ground for you to see. They'll be back soon.*

'Will they?' His eyes are resting on Finula.

We give him tea and biscuits. We don't falter, even though we're afraid. We ask him what he does with himself.

'I'm a faith healer,' he says.

We all smile at each other. We've never had one quite like him before, but then again, we know that, in the end, men are all cut from the same cloth —quick to smile their teeth at us, quicker still to bite.

'Are you believers?' he asks us.

If you prove the power of your god, we might believe you, we say.

He smirks, like he's thinking he can change our minds.

'I saw your prayer tree outside,' he says.

Oh, it's not a prayer tree, we tell him. *Not like how you think, anyway. The well belongs to the goddess of the soil, and with the clooties she keeps us safe, and fed.*

'No one would ever hurt such gentle girls as yous,' he whispers.

So, why is it you're walking through a county as remote and barren as ours?

'I've been after a clutch of women similar to the ones I see before me,' he says.

9

We laugh. We are feeling bolder, but none of us gets too close to him. We still wear scars from the last times we were touched.

'And when will your husbands be back?'

Oh, never. How could they come back from where they've gone?

For the first time, we see a flicker of fear in his lips.

It is a slip, but Finula is still young, seventeen, and only with us a few months.

We wish they weren't coming back, we say. *Sure, don't they work us to the bone, and poor Roisin's man beats her black and blue. But no doubt you'll be seeing them when they're done digging.*

Roisin nods at the fire.

'The fields I saw were unploughed.' He is half raised out of the chair. 'And the cottages I passed had smashed out windows. While I walked here, I thought everyone must've left and gone to the city.'

Ah, no, your eyes were playing tricks on you. There are still people about. Life is hard, but we're at peace with our ways now.

Finula nods and smiles at him.

His fingers fidget in his lap. We offer him another biscuit.

'Do you see many travellers here?' he asks.

A few. Enough.

Finula kneels at his feet, and he gives her his clean, pure hands because she wants to see the hands that heal the broken. She came to us from the city, small and shivering, marked all over from the blows of a man's quick wrist. Our clooties drew her in, like they do everyone who passes, and we

10

healed her, like we healed ourselves from the wounds our husbands beat into us. We taught her our ways. We showed her the hawthorn and how to tear the strips and tie them. We told her our histories, the men and how we survive. We told her she could stay.

His smile for Finula alone is sharp and wolfish.

'I must touch the flesh,' he says, and we understand what he means. Touch, skin on skin, is power.

We line up with our aches and pains, and one by one we unpeel our jumpers and roll up our trousers. We leave some of our skin covered. A charm doesn't work if you remove it.

Our flesh is rolly, purple tinged, white with the scars of age, of working the land, of our own puckered healing where we sewed skin shut. He says nothing about how not one of us wears a corset or bra.

Finula steps out of her dress. We are glad to see his eyes widen to take in her body, healed by us of all the marks, though the memories are still there under her skin.

'Thought I wouldn't find you, wife?' he says to her. 'Look at the state of you. And you here with these old hags.'

We knew you'd come, we say.

'Oh, you did, did you?' He's standing now, turned on us. His hands are clenched in fists, raised and ready to strike. Finula reaches out and gently uncurls his hand.

Go with her, we say and show him our gap-toothed smiles.

He laughs, shakes his head and yawns. 'All right,' he says. 'All right.'

Finula leads him into the bedroom.

We wait, our breaths shallow and loud in the half dark, only the fire to see the glint of our scissors.

We hear the grunts and cries. We know how it goes. Sometimes it is good to be alone with a man.

In the white of dawn, Finula comes through smiling, hands stained.

We carry the bag with his hands inside through the fields and far away from our home, where they can do no harm. We bury them at the base of the mountain.

Back at the house, we remove his clothes: jumper, shirt, vest, shoes, socks, trousers and underpants. We scrub them in boiling water and douse them in cool, clean well water: priestesses at our cleansing. We wait for the rain to stop and then hang the all the clothes in a row on the line.

When they are bone dry, Siobhan and Maebh cut a thin strip from the ends of each item, making sure they're still wearable, and Roisin ties the strips to the tree.

Finula steps out of her dress and into the underpants, trousers, shirt, jumper and oilskin coat. They fit her like skin.

She smiles with teeth that are sharpened. She looks like us.

Are you hungry? we ask each other.

The table is already set.

Fossils

We are a family or we were one once. We are five adults strung out on the beach like driftwood. Bones sucked dry by salt. Sister, Sister, Mother, Father, me. We are hunting the way we used to hunt. What we call ammonites are really only negatives. We are imprints of ourselves as children, pretending we are ready to legitimise any old scrap of stone. We offer the Benefit of the Doubt, featherweight tread in the sand. The cliffs crumble brown and geometric, Tetris stacks splashed with Space Invader slime. Fulmars nest majestically, not like the kittiwakes with their soap-opera to and fro. My sister calls, vocals chords twisting like kelp. We expert-lean-in, Father lifts his glasses from his nose. We make assessments on ancientness and identity.

In the garage at home or what was once called home there is a bucket, salty and incongruous amongst the paint tins and garden shears. Pebbles colourful when wet, fishing weights like teardrops in your palm. Shells, ammonites, endless spirals. The spines of an urchin pulled from my foot, aged eleven. I cried so much that mother lost her rag. I remember the pink fronds of seaweed in the pools, but I don't remember the rain. I've never been in so much pain.

Sisters come with their baggage, I with mine, more from Mum and Dad. The Volvo is accommodating, but we agree there are limits. We can't agree what they are but we remain civil until dinner, candlelit and quaint in the seafront hotel. I order every living thing you can scrape from the ocean floor and watch it dance across the plate like a bad dream. It isn't the done thing to vomit, but think I might. I can't stomach one bite.

The official topic of conversation over dinner is Catching Up, but is actually the projected failures and anxieties of our parents. We taste the wine, calling our own bluff. I spill a drop of crisp white liquid on my hand and it floods right in. My skin has become porous; I make a note to re-proof myself.

It all gets going then. Starts with gentle jibes, pointed comments. The details are unimportant, but you know the type of thing. One sister bitter about the one that got away, the opportunity that barged right in without knocking, made a big old mess, then left. Ghosts of unborn children scamper under the table, squabbling over scraps. Her bile is viscous but still it leaks through my skin with the wine. The younger one is eager, all-knowing, annoying as hell. I spin on the defensive, dervish-quick. My target is both random and precise. Even as I twist the knife I'm disappointed in myself, but sometimes foresight is not enough.

It transpires Mother and Father have been living apart, erratics marooned either side of the tide line. Just like them to steal our thunder. I am unsure what they want from us, why they brought us here, but we pull our best shocked faces and stop our prattle momentarily. After they tell us this they continue to talk, but I make the rest up in my head. I keep my expression fixed but for gentle ripples of feigned comprehension, an anemone filtering the brine with the subtle movement of soft tendrils. There is a suggestion of affairs long ago and I think they were Dad's, but I allow myself to imagine they were Mum's. One of the children isn't his and it could be me. I hope it's me and I start to analyse everybody's nose shape whilst still maintaining the illusion of focus. Little Sister has started up again, a Jack Russell yapping at gulls.

Walking back to the rental, the tide has peeled back and the beach is a reclining nude that nobody wants to paint. In theory there are more fossils to be found but we see very little. The light is failing and it's not the only one. The night is a thousand spirals tightening their grip.

Grounding

My father's killer eats toast with peanut butter and jam for breakfast. He wears a t-shirt and trainers to work and always checks his hair in the living room mirror before heading out of the house. He lives with a woman—wife? Girlfriend? She's blonde and sometimes wears jumpsuits. They have two kids.

I come here four days a week: Mondays, Tuesdays, Wednesdays and Fridays. I can't come on Thursdays because I have PE first thing and Mum drops me off at the sports field on her way to work. We take her leaking Renault Clio. The roof stores water when it rains, so when we turn corners, I have to hold a towel above the gearstick to stop our heads from getting wet.

My father's killer has a great car. A red Audi parked in the smooth drive off the smooth pavement. It's an interesting choice of colour. It's shiny, looks new. I thought about googling, 'how to cut car brakes'. I could easily do it. You can google anything. But I didn't. The Audi has a toddler seat in the back, but still, it's very impractical for kids. Small and cramped and stylish. Not like Dad's Volvo. There are electric charging points all down the street, next to the smooth pavement. I've seen the Audi plugged in sometimes, 'saving the planet'.

***

I couldn't go to my father's killer's house today because I'm sick. I think I caught it off Sian. She coughed next to me all through history without covering her mouth. I turned in the direction of the window to breathe uncontaminated oxygen. Traffic was at a standstill on the road outside school. I couldn't see anyone injured; just two cars smushed together at the junction, like they were kissing. I was wondering how much disruption my dad's accident had caused, and then Ms Mitchell told me to stop daydreaming and face the front, breathing in Sian's disease. Now I'm missing Ms Mitchell's lesson on the feudal system because I have a cold, which serves her right.

I have to go back to school tomorrow, Mum says, because she can't take another day off work unless she really has to. I wrote my own sick note, like always, so that it doesn't contain spelling mistakes, and Mum signed it. Once, my form tutor called her. He thought I'd forged the note to bunk off, but Mum explained that she'd told me to write it, that I did it with her permission. She didn't say any more than that, and as if I'd bunk off anyway. Shows how much they know.

***

After school, I went to church. It was empty. 4.20 p.m. on a Tuesday is God's downtime. But I like it empty. I went to the third row from the front (first row is a bit keen, further back is slacking) and dumped my bag on the pew. When I was a kid, I used to pretend the Bible shelf was a road and raced imaginary cars down it. As long as I wasn't too noisy, Dad didn't mind.

I put down the cushion thing and kneeled; the rubber of my school shoes squeaked as I curled my toes under my heels. I like the quiet, and the smell.

God didn't show up, though. I closed my eyes and leaned over my imaginary race cars and said, 'Dear God—if you're real—please help me. I promise I'll believe in you from now on if you do.'

I waited like that for a while, but, like I said, I guess it was his day off. I didn't waste money on a candle.

***

Yesterday my father's killer's neighbour spoke to me. I was looking through his window, and she crept up beside me and said, 'Are you all right?' And I said, 'Yeah.' But she kept looking at me like 'yeah' wasn't enough. 'I'm waiting for someone,' I said, and she looked at me like, *Why are you so weird?* and then went back up the steps to her house. All the houses on this street have steps leading up to the front door, and the outside walls are white. You can tell a house is posh if it's got outside steps and white walls. I saw her curtains twitch and knew she was peeping at me through them, nosy bat, but I didn't leave straight away. In the past I would have done, but I didn't now.

***

My father's killer's name is David Rose. It's a nice name. Very English and solid. A zebra crossing of consonants and vowels. My dad's name is a garble of consonants—z's and w's and y's and r's—all placed next to each other, where they shouldn't be. My dad's name, like mine, is an English frown. He went to Durham University, David Rose. Now he's director of a tech company in Shoreditch that *goes the extra mile for its clients.* I think about that extra mile. My dad was a mechanic, so I guess he did the same. Maybe he fixed David Rose's car once, helped David Rose go *the extra mile* and then ended up where he shouldn't be.

I found out about David Rose when I was going through Mum's filing cabinet looking for him. There was an article. His name and picture were in it. I googled him. In June, David Rose wrote an article about autonomous vehicles for the company website. *They are likely to be of most use on motorways and A-roads,* he writes. *But it is difficult to envisage how self-driving cars will navigate a densely populated area, such as Soho, without the safety features paralysing the vehicle.* I imagine an Audi and a Volvo moments before impact: two vehicles suspended in space and time.

I went there after school one day, to David Rose's tech company. I waited outside for him and then followed him onto the overground, then through surburbia, where he lives. He didn't see me. He had Bluetooth headphones on and was humming, in his own little world.

***

When I was a kid, Dad was desperate to teach me to ice skate. I clung to the sides in terror, edging the

19

blades along the slush. He decided on a new technique: dragging me into the middle of the rink and then asking me to make my way towards him. I turned my head left and right, paralysed by the oncoming traffic. Skaters whizzed past while I inched my way forwards, arms outstretched. When I moved, he edged back so he was always just slightly out of reach.

'I hate this,' I said, unclipping my skates afterwards. 'I don't want to come here any more.'

'You'll never learn if you don't fall,' he said.

After he died, Mum bought me a guinea pig— I guess to soften the blow. It's pretty lame, but I was scared of that thing. Always getting caught between my feet, all claws and teeth. I thought about releasing it once, but it would've been eaten by a cat, or a fox. Even inside, though, it didn't last long.

David Rose's family have two dogs, black Labs, but I don't know what for.

***

David Rose's wife/girlfriend takes their kids to school each morning after he's gone to work. She asks the older one, Ariella, if she has got her homework. The small one just sits in the pram. When they're gone, I get closer to the window and put my hands over my eyes to see inside better. '*I considered reaching out to the family*,' read the article in my mother's cabinet, an interview with aspiring young entrepreneur, David Rose, '*and offering money. But how can money replace the value of a life?*' I think about this, looking at the grand piano on the garden side of his living room, with his family photos on top. There're toys on the carpet: Lego, a soft rabbit, a Hot Wheels race track. A baby gate is on the door to the kitchen.

'Can I help you?'

I turn around, and David Rose's wife/girlfriend is standing in front of me with the empty pram.

I stare at her, frozen.

'Are you looking for someone?' she says.

'I've got the wrong house,' I say and push past her down the street. I kick myself and bite my hand.

***

I've been coming to David Rose's house in the afternoons since then. I told Mum I joined French club. After school, Ariella plays on the smooth pavements a lot, going along on her kick-scooter. The pavement where she lives is flat as ice, except on the corner with the main road where it cracks and wobbles. David Rose's wife/girlfriend comes out sometimes and tells Ariella to stay in view. She, like her dad, likes to go 'extra.'

I stay on that part of the road now, with its cracks and wobbles, looking up the hill at the white houses with their steps. I rub the edge of my shoe over the side of an uneven paving slab. It leaves a black mark.

Ariella's scooter is pink. She's going up and down in her uniform. I wonder what she'll do afterwards, if she'll go inside and eat dinner with her family, her baby brother sitting in a high chair at the table, banging a plastic spoon on a tray. When her dad comes home, maybe they'll play with the Hot Wheels race track. On the weekend he'll take her to the park and teach her to ride a bike without stabilisers, giving her a push from the back to set her off. I wonder how old Ariella is. I wonder if she's six.

She's tempted to go further, Ariella. I can see her stopping herself reluctantly with each push off down the hill, going as far as the hedge, then the fence, then the house next door. I picture her scooting all the way down the hill, to me, the scooter driving itself, front wheel hitting the black mark on the uneven edge of paving slab where I scuffed my shoe, back wheel lifting off into the air, suspended as she falls.

I open my mouth to call out her name. If she's smart, she'll realise I'm her perfect excuse, that I've given her permission. She's probably been told not to talk to strangers, but does another kid in school uniform even count?

'Ariella!' David Rose's wife/girlfriend shouts.

Ariella turns back towards the house. The woman walks down the hill, grabs the scooter handle in one hand and Ariella's arm in the other, dragging her back towards the steps and the smooth pavement and the white walls. I step on the scuff mark for a second, covering it with my feet as I take a last look up the road.

***

At the ice rink, I clip my skates on and wiggle my toes. I sit on the bench waiting for the whistle to blow, and when it does, everyone piles in. Small kids in puffer jackets hold their parents' hands, and teenagers shoot off across the ice. Everyone is shoving and pushing, but I don't push back. I step in, clinging to the barrier. There's a whole line of us, a queue of fear shuffling its way around, gripping the edge like it's the side of a ship that's sinking to the sound of Taylor Swift.

I let go.

If I don't move, I'll be tripped up by people behind me, so I take a deep breath and push off. I'm free, floating, paralysed in space while around me people zoom. I push one foot back, then the other, arms outstretched and fingers splayed as if the friction of the air could hold me up. I try not to look at the people around me. Instead, I inch forwards towards invisible hands, always just out of reach.

The Gestation Period of a Lemon

There is a lemon in my fridge. It has been there since I moved into my flat. The previous tenants must have left it behind, though they were careful to take everything else. It is still in the butter compartment, where I found it. I have piled a crumby slither of butter and tomato purée and some garlic cloves around it. I did not want to throw the lemon away; it seemed like such a waste. But I have not used it either. It is not rightly mine.

The lemon has changed colour several times. I have been here for eight months now, and it has faded from yellow to ochre to brown to grey. It seems to have settled on grey, for the time being. It is beginning to shrink, to fur at the rind. When it turns black, I shall throw it out.

The lemon, when I first arrived laden with bags under my arms and eyes, was enormous. I have never seen anything quite like it; at first I could not be sure it was not a grapefruit. It had pores that spilled a citric perfume every time I opened the fridge, as though activated by movement like the little light at the top by the jar of thick-cut marmalade. I felt strangely sentimental towards the fruit, and guilty for cramming its domain full of spreadable cheese and cocktail sausages and leftover Chinese takeout. I bought a lime to keep it company, but the lime was soon cut and squeezed, and the lemon was, once again, alone.

I don't touch the lemon very often—only to

check that the underside has not gone to mush. That happened once to a potato that sat in my fridge for a year. The bottom turned wet and dark and pulpy, and I never even noticed until an ominous brown juice began to seep over the shelf. I don't want that to happen again.

It has almost halved in size over the last eight months, becoming compact and intricately wrinkled. I am reminded that we are not so dissimilar to fruit. The lemon is beginning to resemble my grandmother. In old age, she shrunk to the size of a nine-year-old girl and wrinkles made a road map of her face. I used to try to read the lines, her lace tablecloth draped over my head, but I was not quite the fortune teller I fancied myself to be, and I could only predict what she would make for dinner because I had already seen it defrosting on the kitchen countertop.

The fridge is beginning to smell. As soon as the lemon turned grey, its pores furred over and it ceased to fill my nostrils with Amalfi oils each time I swung open the door. The fridge smells amniotic, like curdling milk and wafer-thin ham. The lemon is beginning to darken and sag. The hard woody knot at the top of the fruit has sunk inwards, retreating into the leather flesh. I am tempted to reach into the butter compartment, to take out the lemon and toss it into the bin. But I don't—not just yet. I want to wait a while longer to see what it looks like when the skin has turned black and has softened to suede. I take out the bottle of milk and empty it down the drain.

I have had to remove the garlic cloves and tube

of tomato purée from the butter compartment. The lemon looks convincingly murine, and its grey fur is beginning to spread. I had to throw the butter away; it smelled sour, like lemons.

In the interest of food hygiene and personal curiosity, I have decided to wipe away the mould with a damp piece of kitchen towel. It comes away on the paper as charcoal, and the lemon rind beneath is like liquorice. Unrecognisable as fruit. I am infatuated by its alien strangeness, and carefully take it in my palm, place it on a plastic chopping board, draw a paring knife from the knife rack.

The incision is slight, an inch-long cut so that I might glance inside. I let the tip of the knife slide in until it meets little resistance; that is how I know I have penetrated beneath the pith. I do not want to slice it clean in half. There may be spores inside.

Gently, I squeeze the lemon so that the opening gapes enough for me to peer in. The interior, from what I can gather, is largely dry, though there is a small shiver of moisture where the fruit's innards grow too dark for me to see clearly. I hold it up to the light, and yes—yes, there is something wet within. A globular mass, glossy as a stone freshly lifted from the sea. I drag the knife around the equator of the fruit, completing a perfect circle. And then I twist the two halves in opposing directions, as I have seen television chefs do with avocados when they are ripe.

I prise the lemon apart with a juicy, sickening sound that is expelled exclusively from its centre. The surrounding pulp is desiccated, but at its core —where usually, a little star of pips would be—is a baby, no bigger than a five pence piece and viscous, as though fresh from the womb. I can see now that the woody knot, which would have once been joined to an external stem, has been pulled inwards by another stem—attached umbilically to the baby's navel. I place the empty half of the lemon back on the chopping board. The other half—the top half, the half harbouring life—I hold for a long time, watching the baby breathe and writhe.

And then, I don't know why I do it. The lemon is not, after all, mine. But I pluck the babe from its stem, leaving a tiny knot on its abdomen, and place it on my tongue. It is soft and slick like uncooked offal, but its taste is distinctly sour. My saliva glands swell with the acidity. I hear a mewling within my head; I take care not to bite.

I swallow the baby in one enthusiastic motion. There is no need for water; it slips down quite naturally without. I toss the blackened halves of the lemon into the bin, wash the chopping board and knife with hot sudsy water.

***

In the ninth month of my tenancy, I grow bulbous. I am dappled with cellulite. My skin is oily, my odour sharp. And I am reminded that we are not so dissimilar to fruit. Soon someone will slice me open with a paring knife, and I will spill sour juices and give birth to a child that began life not within me, but within a lemon that I found in my fridge.

Birthday

You have a stiff neck. It's like that every morning these days. You're used to it by now. You stare into the shaving mirror. Your face is half-hidden beneath a frothy layer of lather. It's all white and knobbly and slimy. You barely recognise yourself. You look like Santa's Halloween costume. Two grouchy eyes glare back at you. There's a flicker of malice in them, and they seem to shift, ever so slightly, of their own accord. For a second, you think they belong to someone else. Someone nasty. Someone who's sneering at you. Someone who's mocking you. You can feel their loathing in your clenched fists.

After breakfast, you leave your house and walk to the shop. You walk fast. You always walk fast. If you walk fast, it's much less likely anyone will try to talk to you. You don't want anyone to talk to you— not about the weather, or the football, or the election, or even just to say a simple 'hello'. You don't see the point of it. You don't really like other people. They steal your time. They wind you up. They make you want to be anywhere else but here.

It wasn't always like this, though. You used to have lots of friends. They used to really mean something to you, and you used to really mean something to them. But those days are long gone. It's your birthday today and no one has remembered to send you a card. Your windowsill is empty. No one wants to know you. You're about as welcome as a dung beetle's tongue. Even your wife doesn't sit next to you on the sofa to watch TV any more.

You buy a packet of cigarettes. You barely look at the person behind the counter serving you. You don't like to look at people. Not in the eyes. Because whenever you look someone in the eyes, it makes all your nerves go tense. You feel threatened. You feel they are challenging you, like they want to show you how much better than you they are. You feel they see something about you they just don't like. It poisons your insides. You'd like to punch them in the face, but you daren't. You know you wouldn't win. You've always been rubbish at fighting. It's probably just as well you are, or you would have long since been locked up in jail for sure. So, instead you hope they get run over by a double-decker bus. You've become a spiteful, cowardly, friendless loser, and you know it.

On the way back home, something really weird happens. You're striding down the street, minding your own business, when a woman walking towards you suddenly stops and points at you like she's accusing you of something. 'You have a kamu!' she says (or that's what it sounds like she says). 'I can see him there, sitting on your shoulder. He's making your heart ache, and your neck stiff, isn't he?'

You stare at the woman. She looks like some kind of pirate. She's wearing a red headscarf, and a long, bright skirt down to her ankles, with a sparkly shawl draped over her shoulders, and lots of gold coins around her neck. She's more than a little bit disturbing, but at the same time, there's something deeply honest and sincere about her. You can't help being curious about what she just said. You want to ask her more about this 'kamu' thing. But instead you say nothing. You look away and hurry straight on past her.

As soon as you get back home, the first thing you do is google 'kamu' on your laptop. Lots of results come up about a radio station in Texas, but there's nothing about things that sit on your shoulder and give you a stiff neck. You try spelling kamu a few different ways: kamoo, kimoo, kimmu. Finally a link comes up that catches your eye: 'ekimmu'—a spirit of the dead.

You click the link. A webpage loads up. You read every word. And then you read them all again. It's an epiphany. Everything begins to make sense: the reason why you're always in such a bad mood. Why you can't stand talking to anyone. Why you're so bitter and selfish and miserable. And why you wake up every damned morning with a stiff neck. It's because you're possessed by an evil spirit!

The pirate woman was telling the truth. An ekimmu has attached himself to your shoulder, and he's slowly sucking out your every last drop of decency and spitting it away, until only the foulest, most squalid and most wretched part of you remains.

You want to get rid of your ekimmu, but the webpage doesn't tell you how. It only advises you to think good thoughts and do good deeds, and then evil spirits will stay away. But it's too late for that now. You're already possessed. And it seems it was your own fault getting the ekimmu. He was attracted to you because you were never exactly an angel in the first place. (But who is?) You were just a normal guy who happened to be just about unpleasant enough every now and again to catch the ekimmu's attention. And so now he sits on your shoulder and whispers nasty little thoughts into your ear. It could have happened to anyone, really. Maybe there are loads of people out there with an ekimmu.

There's a drawing of an ekimmu on the webpage. He looks like something not even the cat would dare drag in. His body is thin and bent and hungry—you can see all his spindly ribs. His fingernails are as sharp as bayonets, and his teeth are like hypodermic needles. His nose is just a gaping hole, and his ears are like bat wings. There's a desperate look in his eyes, and he's grinning insanely like some kind of sadistic gremlin. You don't know when you first got him. But it can't have been before you were married, or else surely your wife wouldn't have touched you with a barge pole.

You've seen a couple of movies about people who were possessed. You don't want to end up like them: stuck to the ceiling with blue lips and your head rotating 180 degrees. And there's always some priest or other who comes to the rescue and does some kind of exorcism. It always looks totally horrific. You don't really fancy going to an actual priest, telling him you think you're possessed, and asking if he'll do an exorcism. It wouldn't be like it is in the movies. You know it. The priest would probably think you were some sort of nutcase. He'd probably try to get you sectioned. You wish you'd stopped and talked to the pirate woman. You wish you'd asked her to help you get rid of the ekimmu. But she's long gone now.

So, you decide your only option is to take matters into your own hands. You feel a surge of determination in your guts, like you're mustering an army for a battle. You'll get rid of that damned ekimmu yourself. You'll show that demonic little parasite who's boss. But the question is how? You think about what the priests do in the movies. They command the evil spirit to leave the body. They command it over and over with utmost vigour and conviction in their words until the evil spirit finally gets the message.

You clasp your hands tightly together. The muscles in your forearms harden. There's a bead of sweat on your forehead. You start to fire yourself up. How dare this disgusting ekimmu sit on your shoulder! How dare he trash your life for his own sick pleasure! You're like a bull squaring up to the matador. You inflate your chest with a deep breath of air, and then with a booming voice say, 'Evil spirit, you are not wanted here! You have given me nothing but pain and despair. You hate me and you want me to fail. You have isolated me from everyone I care about. You bring me absolutely nothing of any use. Just what is the point of you?'

You pause for a moment. Every sinew of your body is buzzing. Your heart is galloping around in circles. The whites of your eyes are shimmering. And then you continue: 'I refuse to have your negativity in my life any more. I do not need you, and I do not want you. You are no longer welcome here. Now be gone, evil spirit. I command you! Leave my body now and evermore. I cast you out!'

Everything goes as silent as an empty church. A constellation of tiny stars flicker before your eyes. Your head feels as light as a falling leaf. Your chest is rising and falling like you've just run a marathon. You put the palms of your hands on your cheeks. Your face feels different, and you realise that you're doing something that you'd almost forgotten you could—you're smiling. You roll your neck from left to right. All the stiffness seems to have gone. It's like it's evaporated into the air. You don't feel nasty any more, or angry or despondent. Instead, you feel utterly euphoric!

You've never believed in things like evil spirits and exorcisms before, but now you do because now you feel like a new man. Against all the odds, you have succeeded in casting out your ekimmu. It's like having a bale of hay lifted from your shoulders after years and years of lugging it about. You've been set free. You've been reborn. If you ever see that pirate woman again, you'll thank her with all your heart. Your ekimmu has gone; you don't know where. Straight back to hell for all you care.

In the evening, when your wife comes home from work, you surprise her. You tell her you're taking her out to dinner. It is your birthday after all. You dance around like Scrooge on Christmas Day. She wonders what on earth has got into you.

You're at your table in the restaurant. The food is delicious. The wine is perfect. Everything is going wonderfully. Then your wife tells you she wants to go home. 'What's wrong?' you ask.

'I just don't feel myself tonight,' she answers, 'and I've got a stiff neck.'

You gawp at your wife. And that's when, just for a split second, you see me. My body is thin and bent and hungry. My fingernails are as sharp as bayonets. My teeth are like hypodermic needles. My nose is a gaping hole. My ears are like bat wings. I'm grinning insanely like some kind of sadistic gremlin, and I'm sitting on the shoulder of the wife we now share, waving at you.

The Land of Cardboard

We are born the day we die. Or if we're lucky, the day we get arrested. We, the native citizens of Cartolandia, the Land of Cardboard. The Land of Ghosts.

A concrete barrier divides Avenida Vista Alegre in two. It's our only weatherproof wall. It's our only wall made of something other than paper.

Stretching from the south-east to the south-west of rainy São Paulo, Avenida Vista Alegre—Happy View Avenue—could steal several hours of your day. Its traffic was a cruel mix of intense chaos with intense boredom.

As far as my brothers and I were concerned, the slower everyone moved the better. We made our living when cars were still and drivers impatient. Shirtless, barefoot, we'd approach our customers like thieves. If we were spotted before the right time, they'd angrily shoo us away. But if we could make it to a windscreen unseen, if we could soap it and raise our squeegees, half of the time we'd get paid to clean it, and half of the time to disappear.

Things were easier when we were younger. I'm fourteen now. My big brother Guto is fifteen. My little brother Dado is twelve. When we were all too short to reach the driver's window, our customers would always spare us a few cents, a few centavos. Some would give us trinkets, wish us luck. Some would even buy us warm food.

Aline was like that. Watching ten-year-old me

on Guto's shoulders, holding a squeegee and a bar of soap, she asked me where the closest bakery was and promised to meet us there. She caressed our hair and bought us pastries filled with ham and cheese. She said she was studying to become a history teacher. It was while overhearing Aline talk to the baker that I learned we didn't exist. If you're born in a real house, with real walls, you get papers: documents that prove you're alive, that you came to this world on a certain date in a certain place and have certain rights. Amazing things can happen if you have these papers. You can go to school. You can learn how the world works.

Happy View Avenue is our world. We're free here. Several times a week I make my way to Villa Lobos, a buffet restaurant in a nearby street. I stand alone outside the window. I watch TV. Everything I know about the heavens I learned outside that restaurant, watching a show hosted by a tall man with a funny moustache. It's a show about the stars. It's a show about how we got here.

Mum used to love hearing me talk about the cosmos. She'd press her eyes shut, put her arms around me, and lie on the floor of our cardboard home asking for stories.

A soda can on the floor, empty but for the remains of her precious rocks, the smell of burned rubber infesting the place, I'd tell my mother about light. I'd tell her only space itself, as it expands, can move faster than light. I'd tell her everything that exists today was once tinier than a spark. I'd tell her that outside the Earth's atmosphere you would see the sun in a black sky.

Close your eyes and look up. The sun in a black sky.

***

Out of us three boys, Guto is the bravest. The strongest. He promised to get us papers one day, without getting us killed or arrested.

My big brother walks with a limp. Two years ago, the bones in his right foot were crushed by a motorcycle. He was shoved in front of it by one of my customers.

It was my fault and it wasn't.

We hadn't eaten in days. The traffic was at a standstill. I approached a car without being careful and, after pouring soapy water on its windscreen, I began working, oblivious of the driver's protests. Lowering his window, the middle-aged man took the squeegee out of my hand and started cursing me. He called me *favelado*, a boy from the favela. He called me a bum, a crack addict and a criminal.

Within seconds Guto appeared. I was twelve then, my brother thirteen. He gripped the driver by the collar, and with madness in his eyes ordered him to give us back our property. I saw horror in the man's face, followed by violence. The driver opened his door, throwing Guto against the side of another car. He then grabbed my brother by the ears and shoved him, just as a motorcycle was zigzagging between the lanes. The biker, a delivery guy, nearly lost his balance but did not stop, turning only to curse at Guto. My brother screamed in pain as the back wheel crushed his foot.

No one thought of helping us.

I know the sounds on Avenida Vista Alegre. I know what noises don't belong here. One of us, citizens of Cartolandia, screaming in pain—that's just part of the soundscape, like old combustion engines. Like sirens blaring.

***

Our world is a marketplace. We're bartering beings. If we can't trade something, Guto always says, we have no use for it.

Limping, he moves from one cardboard home to another, making deals with our neighbours. He's the best negotiator in Cartolandia. I trust my siblings more than anyone else, but I think Guto is wrong about the value of things.

Looking up at the skies, at the dreamy blue dawn, at the candle-lit dusk, I see light inviting me. The starry night, infinite and imaginary, asks me to come its way. To see the Moon. The Space Station. Mars. Am I gazing at the future or at the impossible? Or are these two the same for me?

My little brother Dado thinks we'll never leave the Land of Cardboard. Not now that Mum is gone. He thinks it's his fault she's not around.

Will I ever be strong enough to tell him the truth?

Three weeks before Mum disappeared, Dado and a driver became friends. Dado is short for Eduardo, but it also means 'dice' in Portuguese. God does not play dice with the world, the man on TV once said. It terrified me, that quote. It made me think the universe didn't want Dado here. Dado's friend was in his fifties. He drove down Avenida Vista Alegre every day. My brother called him 'moço'—young man—despite his age. This made the young man giggle.

From chocolate bars to real toys, that moço loved to indulge my little brother. Guto would confiscate these gifts, and when Mum wasn't around, he'd make deals with the baker and the grocer and turn them into meals. If Mum was around, she'd order Guto to trade them for cash. She needed the reais to buy her rocks.

Long ago, Mum explained to us that she had a disease of the heart, and her little white rocks were the cure. They smelled like burned rubber. Once I asked Mum if I could taste them. She threw me on the ground and smacked me until my nose was bleeding, my cheeks swollen. She would have gone on for hours if Guto hadn't stopped her. Crying, Mum made us swear on her life we'd never touch those rocks.

Whether this is a brain disease or a superpower, I don't know, but I can use the light in my head to protect myself from pain. Being smacked, I didn't cover my face. I looked over my mother's shoulder, at the sun's rays and the blue skies. Thoughts of tomorrow protected me from today. Tomorrow I'll become an astronaut. An explorer of space. A student of the stars.

Dado's driver friend invited him to Parana, a famous amusement park on the other side of São Paulo. None of us had ever been there. We never went too far from Cartolandia. We had sworn to each other we'd never leave this place alone.

My little brother heard our voices inside his head, but failed to resist the images. The speeding roller coaster, the candy-coloured carousel. He said yes to the moço's invitation and didn't tell us a thing.

**

God does not play dice with the world. What could that possibly mean?

Dado vanished. While my curiosity made me look up at the stars, his made him enter the wrong car.

Limping, Guto visited every resident of Cartolandia while I spoke to our customers. Guto was met with sympathy, I was met with suspicion, neither one of us learned anything.

On day four, Mum said she had to go find her son.

On day five, our little brother returned, alone. His clothes torn. Bruises on his tummy, mouth, and neck.

They never went to Parana. They went to an apartment in the outskirts of the city. All Dado remembered was a single bed and a big television showing the Mirror making a speech, denying the reality everyone could see. Wildfire. Smoke. The vanishing green. The greatest rainforest in the world being destroyed.

Twelve months earlier, tiny mirrors appeared all over the country, reflecting the worst in us. The worst of our vulgarities, of our ignorance. These mirrors found each other and merged, creating a monstrous being. A monstrous Mirror.

Furious, Guto shouted at our little brother he was the dumbest, most pathetic little kid in the world, before crying and hugging him on the floor of our cardboard home.

I looked up and imagined black holes colliding billions of light-years away. I thought of home and saw our galaxy, the Milky Way. I remembered the man on TV explaining how a day on Venus lasts longer than a year, how ironclad Venus, the symbol of love and beauty, spins backwards around the Sun.

Venus is my kind of rebel because a day *does* feel longer than a year. Because everyone—even my brothers—seem to be looking one way while I'm looking the other.

Dado was back. Mum was still gone.

With her, the rescue procedure was different. We had been taught to wait. We had been told she'd always come back to us.

A week later, when we got word she was in the Casarão, I had a very bad feeling. The Casarão—the mansion—was a tiny abandoned apartment where people with Mum's disease went to smoke their rocks. Frightened, my big brother and I went to get her. To hug her. To tell her Dado had come back home.

I walked slowly behind Guto, my eyes locked on his weak foot, my heart hurting. We didn't notice the little mirrors around us, desperate to reflect the worst in us. Inside the Casarão, we found Mommy's lifeless body on the dirty floor of what was once a living room. Her eyes and arms wide open.

Like Pietà.

Staggering, I wanted to use the light in my head. I wanted to find a way out of the world of pain, but the streets of São Paulo wouldn't let me focus. Were those car horns or police whistles? Fireworks or bullets? Screams of joy or hatred?

Guto and I couldn't breathe. We walked down Avenida Vista Alegre, towards Cartolandia. I didn't understand why government supporters were demonstrating. They had won a year ago. Why take to the streets to signal their devotion?

All I wanted was to look up. At the skies, the stars, the universe. But smoke from the Amazonia, our beautiful rainforest, had enshrouded São Paulo.

And all I saw was him.

Our Monster.

Our Mirror.

Curious Tom

Tom once told a journalist that his remarkable journeys were motivated by pure curiosity about the hidden places of Earth. That was true, but he also valued the simple life and increasingly sought it out in his expeditions. As time went on, his style became purer, more minimalist.

He could never have found the path into the Hidden City in his earlier days. The early trips had been exercises in logistics on a grand scale. He would put together a team of six or twelve travellers—chosen for their special skills and robust temperaments—find sponsors and buy equipment, sketch out plans and arrange meetings to discuss contingencies. In those days, he used to say that his trips were like puppet shows, with the real working parts hidden from public view. The journey lasted a few weeks at most, but the preparation would require months or even years. He had to hire local porters to carry everything, which was a particularly demanding business. Sometimes there had to be a series of different teams of porters to carry gear and supplies through different stages of the trip: one for climbing through the mountains perhaps, one for taking boats down the river, one for hacking through the rain forest. Sometimes each successive tribe required Tom to engage a new set of guides in addition to the porters in order to pass through its territory, even when no real guidance was required. Often enough what Tom called his baggage train outnumbered and overshadowed the expedition proper. They brought back samples and specimens in boxes, and sometimes it seemed altogether too much like a military raid, he confessed to Johnson.

'Too *conspicuous*,' he said, 'too alien. I want to become part of the country, not invade it.'

Johnson was the only constant in Tom's expeditions, always closely involved, though he never once left London. It was Johnson's role to be each expedition's home base—the person to whom communications and finds were sent. As well as a regular weekly despatch, Tom wrote endless notes for Johnson, which were meant to be the basis for books that never got written. In Tom's eyes, these sets of correspondence were conversations, although Johnson was rarely able to respond to despatches—and sometimes did not receive them until the expedition had returned home—Tom always felt there was a dialogue. It helped him a lot to think of Johnson's dry commentary and gentle wit, though given the difficulties of communication he usually had to imagine them, only discovering months later what Johnson had actually said. Early in their partnership, Johnson had made a remark that set the tone.

'I've got you pegged, mate. This curiosity of yours. You aren't really trying to find anything. You're trying to get lost.' Tom laughed, but he remembered it.

On the collapse of Tom's third marriage, his wife said he had a closer relationship with Johnson than with her; in fact, the two men did not set eyes on each other for long periods at a time.

Sometimes, Tom was surprised by how much older Johnson looked each time they met, but after the Perna expedition, a much bigger shock awaited him. Johnson had had a sudden heart attack. Tom's constant interlocutor, the man with whom he had been having such lively discussions during recent weeks, had been dead for the last eleven months. This naturally led to a period of silence between them. But Tom's habits were formed, so after a while, he began addressing his despatches to Johnson again. Miss Peregrine, the young woman who took over the liaison role and worked tirelessly to put Tom's papers into publishable form, never commented on this.

It was to Johnson, of course, that Tom first confessed how unhappy he was with the size of his early expeditions, and with the bearers and porters in particular.

'It seems wrong that I should be claiming the ascent of Mount Pinobar as some kind of personal, egotistical achievement,' he said, 'when there are twenty people who worked harder and showed more skill in forwarding my expedition. The other thing about these baggage trains, Johnson, is that they make such a fearful racket, and carry so much trash about. I prefer to move quietly and leave no tracks behind me. And then one has to deal with all their problems, too. There's so much gossip and petty jealousy on some of these trips that I really might as well be spending my time in that bloody village in Suffolk where I believe my last wife lives.'

Tom's response to his own concerns was to begin paring down his trips. Increasingly, he travelled solo, and he made do with simpler equipment. He learned to live off the land, hunting and foraging as he went, so that he could manage with a much smaller stock of supplies. This style of travel would not serve in the Arctic or the great deserts, of course, but in the forest it worked well. He no longer needed much in the way of funding, and his preparations became shorter and simpler.

'My ultimate aim,' he told Johnson, 'is to reach the point where I can simply walk into the forest in my shirt sleeves, and keep going for as long as I like, wherever I want to go. I think it's attainable. People live in these places, comfortably; always have.'

He was close to achieving this ideal when he set off on his search for the Hidden City; he took only a small rucksack full of notebooks.

'I know you have called this my El Dorado trip,' he told the long-dead Johnson in one of his despatches, 'I understand what your sly references to the local bats are meant to imply. But you know quite well it is nothing of the kind.'

The confused legend of El Dorado might attract its share of the batty, but the story of the Hidden City was relatively prosaic. It was said that deep in the forest there was an ancient metropolis, neither ruined nor abandoned but living and working as it had done for many centuries. It was hard to find, but some said that on a certain known outcrop in the deepest forest, in the morning and evening, travellers occasionally heard the distant voice of a priest calling out from a tower high above the vaulted treetops—a sound like a lost muezzin. No traveller was known to have come any closer to the city, for below the outcrop was an impassable ravine that barred the way.

'I don't know why it should be,' Tom told Johnson, 'but that distant call has piqued my curiosity greatly. You recall that I heard it seven years ago when passing through on my way to the Acu Valley. The sound had a distinct quality no sound has ever had for me—that of a destination; I might almost say a home. It spoke of a place in my long-gone past. It goes without saying that I believe in the city absolutely and discount all other explanations for that distant cry.'

A week later, he reported that he had made frustratingly little progress with his search.

'But in my quest to become a man of the forest, I am succeeding admirably,' he said. 'I have very largely ceased to trap animals, or to fish, and have become instead almost a strict vegetarian. It is in many ways simpler, and I am increasingly convinced it is healthier. It does require some skill in tree climbing so that one can reach the best fruits, but I have become very nimble among the branches. At times I find it advantageous to pass from one fruit tree to another without setting foot on the ground at all. I have also made great strides in my woodcraft. Yesterday I passed close by an Indian standing in the forest without his being aware of me at all. I could have reached out and plucked an arrow from his quiver. I must report, however, that there are signs of unexpected developments going on behind me, of a kind I shall have to investigate and address if I am to return.'

Two weeks later he wrote in great excitement that he had reached the edge of the road network which he believed surrounded the Hidden City. From here, the howling call of the presumed priest each morning and evening sounded clear, though still at some distance.

'Of course, these roads are mainly paths set high in the tree canopy,' Tom explained. 'The citizens have certainly found that it is faster and more convenient to travel between trees, as I too have found at times. Yesterday, on one of these roads, Johnson, what I take to have been three true city dwellers looked down on me from far above! A negligent young fellow leaned on a sort of rail up there and pointed me out to his companions. I am, it seems, of little concern to them; they laughed and strolled away before I could get a good look, but I am greatly encouraged.'

Now, he determined that, like the roads, the city itself sat high among the trees for the most part.

'And why not?' he asked. 'We are, of course, the heirs of the Romans in this respect. We look for stone as the marker of civilisation. Yet our own ancestors built in wood. You asked for more information about the developments that I said have occurred behind me, but please contain your impatience. I am not in any danger. However, it is becoming clear that I am going to have to improve my climbing skills somewhat, and I have resolved to sleep and travel in the trees as much as I can from now on, as the locals seem to do. The citizens have come once again to stare at me from a distance, but I am still only in the thinnest suburbs of this mighty conurbation. They smile and seem friendly, but no deputation has come forward. Tomorrow I shall be passing between their dwellings at last, and I must devise some kind of greeting. Every morning now I hear the priest calling from his high tower, clear and strong and close at hand. "Come home!" he cries, "come home!"'

The last despatch is stained and a little difficult to read. Given his limited supply of notebooks and the need to carry them all with him until he could reach some outpost of civilisation, Tom wrote in tiny letters and crammed each page with text.

'I have now investigated the developments to the rear, Johnson, and I am afraid there is no doubt about their nature and their growing extent. I shall not be able to return as I came—or, indeed, at all. I will be obliged to leave these despatches in a tree. I shall do my best to place them safely, but I am afraid it is almost certain they will perish without ever being seen by you—or I suppose I should say by Miss Peregrine, whose indulgence I must beg. But please don't think I feel regret: quite the contrary. You see, I have indeed reached the destination my heart desires. I have been concealing certain matters from you. Things have progressed more than I have said. I have not mentioned, for example, that the citizens here go naked and, to promote my acceptance, I discarded my clothes some weeks back. As for those rearward developments I have mentioned, I tell you plainly now, Johnson, once and for all, that I am growing a

49

tail. Today I enter—joyfully and permanently—the City of the Monkeys.'

A Bell, a Step, a Cry

A bell rings. A step falls. A cry splits the silence.

Helena lies and she listens.

Every afternoon it's the same. Muffled, soft behind the wall that joins her house to its neighbour, the ring, the step, and then the cry. At first she had to listen out for it, catching the sound only faintly beneath the radio's gabble or the dishwasher's hum. Now she hears it wherever she is, no matter what else she is doing. Folding laundry in the kitchen. Packing up toys in the bedroom. The bell, the step, and then the cry; the cry that is not quite a word, that is sometimes a song and is often, surely, a name being called.

Helena lies on the pullout bed, and she listens. She pictures an elderly woman or somebody sickly —a frail person, small and paper-skinned. They are calling for water; they are ringing for help. Perhaps they cry out in their sleep, and that's why the words sound so strange. Perhaps they are lonely, or even afraid.

Jacob tells her she must try to get out. Just to the shops, he says, to pick up the paper. Just to the café for a coffee-to-go. And then you can come right back, he says, like being at home is a treat she must earn.

But he's gone more than he's there, so he doesn't hear the bell or the cry. At first, Helena is glad of this because it's like a secret between her and the high ceilings and the teddy-papered walls. Only she knows that it will come, and she cradles the knowledge, strolls around the house with it, waiting, and smiles to herself at the first distant ring of the bell. If there were ever a visitor or someone else with her, she'd lift a finger to her lips when it started, to show that they should listen. Every day, she'd say, with a knowing shrug. Every day I hear it.

After the hospital, though, she wishes that Jacob would hear the sounds too, because the bell is the same and the step always falls straight after, but the cry, she's sure, has changed. On weekends when Jacob is home, she orchestrates reasons for them both to be upstairs. She speaks softly, moves only a little. And when it begins, she makes sure to be silent, and she watches his face, watching for his hazel eyes to widen and for the fall of his gentle mouth.

First the bell, ringing quite clear on the other side of the wall. Then the step: one quick footfall, heel then toe, across uncarpeted floor. And then of course the cry; the cry that she's sure has changed. 'Did you hear that?' she wants to say, but instead she waits and watches.

His expression is flat. He has not heard, has not recognised, does not understand. He only repeats the question he asked her before: 'What will we do with all these things?'

Helena lies and she listens. Her house adjoins its neighbour on the corner of a square—all early Victorian, three-storey sorts. Their front windows face onto grey cobbled courtyard. If she stands at the right angle, pressing her cheek to the glass, she can see into next door's windows. But the curtains are always drawn, and she never sees anyone enter or leave, even when she watches for hours.

In winter the days are so short that it doesn't seem worth getting up. Helena can smell herself on the mattress: unwashed hair, pungent skin. Days of bleeding. Months of salt. She tells time by the ring of the bell breaking the throbbing silence, by the peal of the cry. 'I can hear you,' she calls. 'Are you there?'

The bell, the step, the cry. Is somebody suffering? Are they in pain, are they hurt, are they frightened? Helena flattens her hand against the wall. Could someone be dying in there just a few feet away? Are they calling and wondering why help doesn't come? And whose foot is falling on that hard wooden floor, and why is it only one slow step they take? If it were her, she would fly to that sound; she would hammer up the stairs, knocking frames off the walls. She'd make thunder through the house just to reach it.

She lies and she listens, and when she sleeps, she hears it still: long and sorrowful and faltering. In her dream it ebbs on and on, birdsong on a wave. It's a greeting and a parting, and a taking of weight from her arms.

Helena wakes to a sound from her own mouth —a deep animal moan, a lowing like a dairy cow. Her arms are clutched around herself, her fingers digging in.

The bell, the step, the cry. No matter how deep her sleep, she wakes on the minute to hear them. She moves round the house on tiptoe, unplugging the phone and lifting her head often, like a dog waiting for a whistle. She is afraid to miss it, afraid this might be the time that she finally makes out the sound, hears the word in the whimper. Was that it? She snatches the kettle from the stove to stop its whistle. But no—only a bicycle passing outside. And then? Just the sound of the heating coming on. She stands rigid, clenched in the empty centre of rooms. She stops eating, for the volume of her chewing is too loud. She presses her hand up to Jacob's mouth when he speaks. All she wants to do is listen.

And one day she wakes and hears nothing at all.

She sits up, blinks back the clots in her vision. The silence gapes, rings, presses into her ears. As she strains to listen, her hands grasp the grubby sheets, her eyes stare wild and white at the wall. She clicks her fingers to make sure she has not gone deaf. Has she missed it? Slept through it? Or have the sounds not come at all today?

Helena waits for a long time. The silence is thick, suffocating. She feels she can't draw enough breath. She gets up from the pullout bed, her limbs stiff and sore, and clambers into a dressing gown several sizes too big. She edges around the rocking chair, picks across a floor scattered with clothes and papers and mouldy plates. Slips into a pair of Jacob's shoes.

Outside, the day is blustery, and there's snow in the wind. Helena's head rings with cold, clean air. The courtyard is empty. Her neighbour's door is not locked.

Inside it is quiet, and there is a thin musty smell, the smell of rooms left closed up for too long. When Helena tries a light switch, nothing happens. She calls out and nothing moves, no bedsprings groan, no footfalls above.

The house is a mirror of her own. She is careful climbing the staircase, making sure not to creak, her gaze trailing over the lighter patches on walls where pictures once hung. There's a buzzing up her spine, the same feeling she gets in attics and the side rooms of churches—that sense of a presence unseen and ancient.

And when she reaches the landing, Helena hears the bell.

She turns as it peals, spins on her heel to see that it is only a clock after all.

The bell, after all, is the chime of a clock. A grandfather clock in the hall. Its hands point to the wrong hour—to one, not to two. Perhaps it has not been wound in a while, or dust has built up in the mechanism; either way, the time is lost. The bell has rung.

Helena wonders why it is set to ring only once in a day and at this time, and why no other. She steps towards the clock with her hand outstretched, but then she stops. For then there comes the cry.

It comes from along the hall. It comes from behind a door along the hall, towards the front of the house. It comes from behind a door that bears a single initial, a capital T, which Helena touches with a fingertip. Tim, Thomas, Tilly. A monogram. This, she thinks, is a child's room.

Hope flares, nonsensical. Unbearable. A child's room. A baby's cry.

But within there is no cradle. The walls are not papered in gambolling bears or bright yellow ducks. There are books on the shelves but they're leather bound, bearing difficult titles in miniature fonts. It's a shabby sort of study, or a half-hearted library—a dim little room devoted to files and paperwork. A cracked leather chair stands by the fireplace. And behind the chair, on a barley-legged table, is a cage. And inside the cage is a parrot.

On seeing Helena it tips its white-fringed head to one side, clicks, trills an inquisitive whistle. It shakes its feathers, puffs its chest, dips its head. And then it cries again.

So soft and sad, the cry. So sweet and so familiar. It is a word, but not a word that anyone knows, and how this parrot has it she can't understand. But here it is again: that one little wail she thought she'd lost, that saying hello and that calling goodbye.

Helena walks to the window and pushes the curtain aside. From here she can see across the courtyard and, if she stands at the right angle with her cheek pressed against the glass, into her own home. From here she can see the mattress of the pullout bed, pushed askew from her hurried leaving. She can see the tangled pillows, the tossed-aside sheets, the empty rocking chair. From here she can see the place where she'll sit and she'll listen, knowing now that it's only a bird.

Unexpected

He's here, well on his way. Down the hall I wait, my ears subconsciously know the time and strain, listening out for his familiar cacophony, the sound that surrounds and trails after my strange visitor.

Step, drag, tap.

Step, drag, tap.

He whistles, a sign he is in a good mood; he must have found a pound on the pavement, or a fiver in his coat pocket, or he's heard from his granddaughter who moved to Canada. It's the little things he takes pleasure from: I never got that before. Time sped up, then little things got lost and trampled.

I think how similar we are now, in our ways. For one, neither of our families bothers with us any more. Time and distance does that to relationships. My sister was the last. She had dyed her hair 'red,' she said.

What kind of red?

Did she do it herself or go to that posh salon in town?

What did Mum think? Questions reeled off one after the other but were contained within.

I felt full. Like after a Sunday lunch carvery.

Ohh, what I would give for some roast beef and Yorkies. I haven't had them in ages.

I wanted to feel her hair, run my fingers through the strands. Was it coarse and brittle or smooth like silk?

I'm forgetting the infinitesimal details of

colours and texture. I wish she'd leaned her head down to my hand; I wish I could know if maybe she did.

'Hello me duck.' He shuffle-taps his way to my bed. 'How's thee today? You'll never guess …'

He pauses for dramatic effect. I try to smile for him.

'There was a *Metro* on the bus just now—last one, too! Left from this morning I suppose.' The sound of a plastic carrier bag scrunching and shuffling paper is the background to his words. So, this was it: a free newspaper. My senses have been heightened while I've been here, bringing memories surfacing from some forgotten depth, like that ambitious class project to make a paper mache dinosaur at school. To my five-year-old self, it was life size.

He reads the horoscopes first. He doesn't know it's my birthday, so he reads them all, commenting as if each one is relevant to me specifically.

'Oh, says 'ere you'll come into some money by end of week. All right for some.' That was Sagittarius.

'Oh, look. Says you'll be disappointed by someone close. Never you mind their loss, love.'

He's a Capricorn; his luck is changing. I'm a Leo. A career opportunity will present itself at the end of the month.

With a few crackled flips of the page, he reads sports, celebrity gossip and politics.

'Nuke 'em all, I say.'

He also doesn't rate the article about eating too

much red meat.

'What next? Can't eat nowt without somebody with too much time on their hands tellin' you ain't no good.'

I wonder if he has a wife, one that cooks for him and presses his shirts and trousers, pats down a rouge tuft of hair before kissing his forehead. But somehow that image doesn't fit, so I decide that he's been a widow for at least ten years and that he's not the pressed-trouser kinda guy. It's also the smell he carries with him: his own cloud of earthy unfreshness, like he hasn't washed in a couple days, but neither have I, so I don't judge. He's finished with the paper; it goes back in the bag. Then it's the banana.

Another memory. Baking with my aunt, we added walnuts, chocolate chips and cinnamon to the batter, evenly dividing the mixture with an ice cream scoop into hot-pink silicon muffin cups.

I've come to expect the sound of splitting peel and the sweet smell. I can taste it. I want a bite, I want a lot of things, but instead I rely on my imagination and memory and sitting at the kitchen table with Donna eating our fresh-out-the-oven banana muffins.

The nurse comes in to chat to him. She comes back a couple minutes later and puts a cup of tea on my side table.

'Cheers chick,' he says. He's a slurper, but even this I don't mind.

My expectations and standards for human interaction have drastically shifted. Similar to when I did internet dating back then. I started with high expectations: a long list of desirable features and attributes. I went to a workshop one Saturday and made a vision board. I read *The Secret*. I visualised my future. Put out positive vibes. I was proactive, but then when that didn't work, I loosened my grip on the fantasy and scratched all but a few essentials. A couple months later, the vision board went in the bin, and by the end of the year, finishing a pint of Ben and Jerry's Double Chocolate Fudge Brownie in one sitting was no longer a challenge.

I think now how my life has simplified to the point where a slurping man is no longer an issue.

A lot of things set me off now that didn't before. There's a consultant who comes once a week. He explains my vitals to medical students. Leaning over me, he tells these invisible people (or person) what's going on. No one else speaks, but I assume he's not alone; it is a teaching hospital, after all. Specks of spit like snowflakes hit my nose, above my right eyebrow, and on the corner of my mouth. I've become more and more disgusted and try to shrivel up inside this cocoon of a body and wait for him to leave. He has stopped introducing me now, whether that's because he's always with the same people or because he can't be bothered, I don't know. As a judgemental person, the instant I saw someone I would make an instant decision about whether I liked them or not and left it up to them to prove me wrong or, as in most cases, right. It must be something that is inherently in me, part of my DNA. I still catch myself doing it now, from the way someone walks into the room with high-pitch of heels or the sticky, muted rubber soles of

Crocs. The way staff check my vitals! Do they apologise for cold hands? Do they tell me they need to hear my chest first before pulling up my gown or do they get right in there, pressing the metal stethoscope to my bare skin?

He's different. An anomaly. The kind of guy you wouldn't make eye contact with if he got on your bus and you have an empty seat beside you. He's a chaotic man, a jolly bundle of riddles and puns. A talker; he talks at you. I guess that's why our relationship works. I'm not sure really what constitutes a relationship, but I've come to rely on these visits as much as I didn't want to. I enjoy them and find reassurance and comfort in them. I know I shouldn't put so much pressure on it, though. It's a candied window, fragile and sweet, easily shattered. I remind myself every time he leaves that it could be the last. I need this bit of control, a safety net. Because if it were true, I'd be alone. I'd fall and keep falling endlessly, forever.

But he does come the next day, and the one after that, and the one after that, and the one after that.

He comes and he tells me about the woman at Tesco who charged him twice for a tin of basic baked beans and called the manager over to prove that she was right and that the old timer didn't believe her and wouldn't let up over a twenty-pence tin of beans. They took all his shopping out, to the outraged tutting of the customers in the queue behind him. But one tin of Tesco Value baked beans was all they found. The manger, slightly embarrassed, apologised and let him have the beans at no charge and called the café to tell them he could have a complimentary coffee.

Last week, he read three brochures on Jehovah Witnesses he was given by a couple of women stood outside the town hall. 'They seemed nice, but I told 'em I'm not interested in any of their God stuff.' The brochures were all pretty much the same, but we persevered to the final copyright, editor and publishing names.

He usually stays for two cups of tea. On one of our visits, he told me he preferred the taste of coffee but the caffeine kept him up too late. I wanted to suggest he try decaf, but I didn't, and I stayed silently still. My mind wanders while he talks. His stories are sometimes hard to follow, too detailed, and he uses names of people and places I've never heard of or been to.

My mum came right after the accident. She did her motherly duty and stayed by my bed for three days until I started breathing on my own and was moved up here. She spoke to the doctor in a hushed, angry voice. They closed the bed curtain. Whoosh—metal rings pulled along the metal pole, a quick movement.

'She's lucky to be alive Mrs Dunbar.'

'It's *Ms*. And what kinda life is that?'

'Motorcycle accidents rarely have survivors, especially in these circumstances. The driver went straight into the oncoming car's windscreen, killing them both instantly.'

'That idiot! I knew something like this would happen. I told her hundreds of times not to get on that death trap, especially not with Mr Boy Racer.'

Daryl is dead.

We'd not been going out that long—a couple months, eight weeks maybe. It was young love, a spend-every-minute-together love, bunking-off-college love, pissing-my-mum-off love.

That day is a black blot. Sometimes I think I've got hold of a piece, a corner that I can lift up so I can see it, remember it. But then, like when we stripped the wallpaper in the back bedroom, the corner comes away, but the rest just stays glued down. I need a steamer like we had then. I wonder if electric shock therapy would work and jolt the pieces together.

Do they give that to coma patients?

'Right me duck, that's me off.' A chair scraps the floor and knocks the table, rattling the cup and saucer.

'See you when I see you,' he says. His usual farewell is curious, like he doesn't know if he'll be back. It takes the pressure off anyway. His shuffle-tap fades, see-yous are exchanged at the nurses' station, then he is gone.

Saint Perfect

Our first night together in Rome, my brother Franky tells me the latest gossip. 'Spit it out,' I tell him, and he does. First off is the undocumented Ghanaian migrant currently living in his apartment. 'The camp was right down the street from me, but the police tore it down and threw everyone's crap in the dumpster—tents, blankets, the works.' Shaking his head, he reaches for the bread basket. 'It was like they enjoyed it, those savage fucks.' When he saw it on the news, Franky headed there straight away—'to see if I could help out and shit.'

Oko, Franky's Ghanaian roommate, is twenty years old. He spends a lot of time watching Rhianna videos on his phone. He loves dancing, and American music, and Asian action movies. He wants to get a tattoo like Jay-Z and has asked Franky repeatedly if he knows of any affordable tattoo shops in the neighbourhood. He can't read or write, because his father didn't think it was important to send him or any of his nine siblings to school. Back in Ghana, he worked as a taxi driver. But he's been in Italy for three years now, working in the Sicilian fields, picking tomatoes. He speaks no Italian but he and Franky communicate in broken, gesturing English. According to Franky, he was initially worried about leaving Oko on his own for six days—'It was guilt, man. Me tramping around Rome with my big brother, keeping him company on his big ole fancy book tour, while this poor dude who can't cook just starves to death in the guest bedroom!' But when Franky asked him

64

about it, Oko just replied cheerily, *Oh, don't worry. If I survived Libya, I can survive anything!*

'Why, what happened in Libya?' I drink the last of my wine too quickly. An enormous plateful of salami and ham still awaits my attention. Franky insisted on ordering it for me, despite my mumbled refusal.

'He hasn't told me yet—but I'm sure it was nothing good.' Franky lets out one of his screeching laughs, the kind that makes me wince and look around anxiously, in case anyone else is watching. Franky never looks, though. Franky doesn't care.

This has always been Franky's big thing— gestures, I mean. Vegetarianism, veganism. Arguing with teachers. Arguing with Jehovah's Witnesses. Arguing with our middle school Christian classmates about why *Will & Grace* wasn't sinful. He appears briefly on Wikipedia, in the article about Occupy Wall Street. Once, during a pro-Ralph Nader dinner table debate, he made our father so mad he frothed at the mouth.

Saint Perfect—that's what our father used to called him, before thwacking him on the back of the head with the bread knife. But Franky would just smile. Our father's rages made my stomach gurgle, sit on my hands to stop them from shaking, duck my head. But Franky always sat up tall.

Franky is going to buy Oko a ticket back to Ghana. They've both agreed it's the best solution. Oko doesn't have a passport, but Franky has sent money via Western Union to Oko's friend-of-a-friend in Accra, to pay the application fee. 'It's definitely gonna be a fake document, but better than nothing, right?' Oko has shown Franky footage on YouTube of his village—unpaved roads, men on bikes holding onto the backs of trucks, etc. 'He's just a kid, basically. Jesus, here I am, living with someone fifteen years younger than me. We should go clubbing!' He waves down the waitress, speaking to her in rapid Italian with no discernible accent. 'Another bottle of red is fine, no?' He doesn't wait for me to answer.

Franky is planning to accompany Oko to Barcelona, in order to ensure he makes his connection. Because Oko can't read, Franky is concerned about him making it through customs. 'It's amazing that he's gotten this far, really—talk about life skills. They don't teach that shit at Harvard Business School!' It doesn't help that Oko doesn't have the document he was supposed to have been given by the immigration police in Sicily, a slip of paper stating the date and time of his arrival. Without this paper, Oko can't apply for asylum. 'But even if he did have it, it wouldn't matter, 'cause he gave the immigration peeps a fake name and birthday anyway. Isn't that nuts? Paperless! He's a paperless person!'

Franky takes out his rolling tobacco, offering me some, but I shake my head—around Franky, I pretend like I've quit. An insignificant moral victory, I know. But with him, I have to take what I can get.

'You should write about this,' I say as he raises the rollie to his lips to dampen it. 'For a newspaper, or something.'

He raises his eyebrows—dark and bristly, just like mine. Our only shared physical feature. 'Dude… nobody wants to commission an article about Oko.' He snorts. A small flake of brown tobacco flies out the rollie and onto the table. 'Nobody gives a shit about his story. And in any case, you're the writer, not me.'

I don't reply.

Franky likes to talk about the possibility of authentic assistance. He talks about the totalizing effects of neoliberal capitalism, 'how it creeps into absolutely-fuckin' everything, like the worst kind of jizz stain.' He talks about how the last remaining sites of hope in this fucked up world are the small interactions between individuals. And even if it's not exactly hope, at least it's something a teensy tiny bit different than despair. Franky's given up on large-scale systems of justice—that's what he tells me while filling our glasses of wine halfway, as opposed to the brim like I would (in this way and many others, I truly am my father's son). Franky says it's the small moments in our daily lives we have to cling to—relationships and exchanges between two people. Communication that isn't based on profit or domination or tearing everything down, like the police sweeping countless shantytown tents into the trash.

I don't say, *But Oko is just a faceless, vague figure in your dinnertime anecdote. An anecdote you're narrating right now as a source of entertainment. How are you not profiting from that?*

I also don't say: *And how is it not a form of domination, in terms of who gets to speak about who, and in what way?*

I don't say this, because I don't say what I'm ever really thinking to Franky. Even in my own writing, my primary aim (duty, even) is to entertain. So instead, I fill my mouth with wine.

Oko *has* cooked at Franky's, to be fair. Chicken in peanut sauce. Rice. Instant noodles. Franky tries to keep the apartment well-stocked, but it's hard since he prefers eating out. 'No shortage of that here in Rome, as I'm sure you can imagine!' For this book tour trip with me, he left Oko with some cash, a friend's phone number for emergencies, and instructions to put the garbage out on Wednesday. 'I had to show him how to do it, but that's fine. He's a bomb-ass roommate overall—the best I've ever had.' He carefully places his well-made rollie next to his glass of water for later—unlike our father and I, the perpetual puffers, Franky only smokes after coffee, pre-rolling his cigarettes well in advance. 'In the tomato picking fields, he slept in one room with twelve other people. And then the managers kicked him out for missing curfew, the bastards. So dystopian.'

My seafood pasta arrives—Franky's gone for what looks like roasted vegetables on sticks, vegan skewers. 'Yum!' he squeals, digging in right away. Franky chews with his mouth open, smacking his lips, a lifelong childhood habit. Jauntily, not a care in the world. Meanwhile, I put my napkin on my lap, tuck it into my shirt collar, put it back on the table. Anxious and fretting, my hands flitting and fussy. *Stop moving around like a fucking fairy*—that's what my father liked to say.

As I mix the spaghetti around in the red sauce, I think about it. Had Oko's hands touched any of the tomatoes in the sauce? What about the tins I bought back home in the U.S.? The ones from at my corner shop Brooklyn co-op? Or had they been handled by the Hondurans, the Salvadorians, the Mexicans? Why couldn't this information be included on the label, along with calories and the organic/non-organic label?

It's tempting to feel like this curiosity is profound—evidence of my deepening, more thoughtful and profound character. But the very fact that I'm making it about me at all is just further evidence of the separation between me and Franky —he would know the right thing to think, to feel, to believe. He would never use the phrase 'the right thing to think,' for example. And if there's anything potentially icky about the way he's talking about Oko—inappropriate or offensive—I'm not smart enough to put it into words.

As I use the last of the bread to mop up the sauce, Franky tells me more gossip. Who's divorced. Who's running for Congress. Who's living a secret life as a private video porn star. Even in Europe, he's more in touch with our classmates than me. I try to get him to discuss Brexit, the behind-the-scenes inner wheelings and dealings, but he instantly shuts down, lips pressing together— ever the consummate professional. Before moving to Rome to freelance, he worked for the EU in Brussels as a translator. He speaks ten different languages, Franky does. A polyglot—I suppose that's what you call them, people like him. A man of many talents, especially when it comes to communicating.

'Tell you what,' Franky says, studying the dessert menu. He orders who knows what, again without consulting me. 'You know what I think you should do? You should write about Oko. Tell his story!'

My middle finger starts scraping at my thumb. I successfully tear away a long strip of bloody skin before I slowly, consciously force myself to stop.

'Think about it,' Franky is saying. 'Put it in one of your crime novels. Oops, I mean thrillers. Are they thrillers or crime? Whatever - you can do it all sneaky-like. Picture the marketing campaign: hidden clues of social justice, for discerning motherfuckers! Commercial fiction, finally making a difference!' He grins balefully, all teeth.

'Suspense,' I say. 'My publisher marketed the last series as suspense.' (This is a lie—to be accurate, they didn't market it at all.)

'Really? I didn't know that was a genre.' He picks up his rollie and tucks it behind his ear. 'It would work, though—I'm basically breaking the law by letting him stay.' He laughs happily, and there's something about that sound, that pure note of delight, that makes my stomach twist. 'If harbouring a fugitive from the law isn't a classic suspense plot, guaranteed to thrill the masses, I don't know what is!'

Moments like these, it's hard not to stare at my little brother. So young and hard and bright. So unabashed about what to say and feel. So certain of his place in the world.

'Goody for you,' I say. He looks at me, just a little too quickly. But I can't stop myself. Not now. 'Aren't you just… Saint Perfect.'

At the sound of my father's nickname for him, Franky's brow furrows. He touches his rollie, as if wanting to make sure it's still there. The bread is all gone, so I use my index finger to wipe up the last of the sauce, licking it clean. It feels appropriate. The kind of gesture a confident, assured person would make. Experimentally, I try smacking my lips, sitting up tall, sneaking a glance to see if he's watching. But of course he isn't. Why would Franky watch me when he's so busy watching himself?

When Franky finally speaks, he speaks quietly. 'I'm not going to do this with you, Louis.'

'Do what?'

'You know what I mean.' Franky's voice is still low, but there's a register there I haven't heard before. Something hard. Or maybe it's sad.

I say, 'You got something on your mind there, Frank? Something you want to say to your dear big brother?'

We look at each other.

'Don't be afraid now,' I say. 'You can say it— what you really think of me.' I laugh happily, clapping my hands. 'Spit it out.'

He bites his lip.

I guess I'll never know what's going to happen to Oko. He'll remain shadowy to me, elusive. Anything I can say about him at this point will feel more like gossip than truth. He's waiting for his passport, I suppose. Waiting for the money to be wired, for the plane ticket prices to go down, to go back to the place he worked so hard to leave. For his life to begin in one way and end in another. And waiting for Franky, most of all. But soon enough I'll be making a move of my own—with the fiercest, most savage joy. The kind you only get when you tear your life down, throw everything away knowingly, and on purpose.

About the Authors

Marmalade—Hannah Whiteoak

Since I was a small child, fiction has brought me a huge amount of joy. I enjoy reading and writing about alternative worlds and wondering, 'what if…?'

Since moving to Sheffield in 2014, I've found communities that have supported and encouraged me to write fiction, including Blank Street Writers and The Kurious Hub, where I am currently taking courses taught by Rosie Carnall and Laura Wake. Writing alongside others is a great source of inspiration and helpful feedback to take a story from messy first draft to polished prose.

I am proud to have stories published in three anthologies with other local writers: *Beyond the Sea* and *The Last House* (Blank Street Writers, 2018 and 2020) and *Taking Flight* (Comma Press, 2019). I am currently working on a personal collection of flash fiction, which I hope to complete in 2020.

Twitter: @HannahWhiteoak

A Healer's Touch—Molly Aitken

I'm a novelist living in Sheffield in an old house that inspires stories about cold and creepy locations. I was born in Scotland in 1991 but brought up in Ireland by a Dublin mother so I'm confused about where I'm really from. My debut novel *The Island Child* is out now with Canongate.

I've won a short story prize and been shortlisted for others. Early in my writing journey, I did an MA in Creative Writing at Bath Spa University. After I graduated, I won the Janklow and Nesbit Prize for an early shoddy draft of *The Island Child*.

When I'm not writing my second novel, I review books, write short stories and personal essays for *Cunning Folk Magazine*. I also edit other writer's novels and ghostwrite memoirs on occasion.

Twitter: @MollyAitken1

Fossils—Genevieve Carver

Genevieve is a Sheffield-based writer searching for the humanity amidst the chaos. She began writing and performing poetry on the open mic. circuit in 2011, and has since gone on to appear at events and festivals from the Edinburgh Fringe to the Canadian Rockies. Her work has appeared in publications including *Iota*, *Envoi*, and *The North*, and her first collection *A Beautiful Way to be Crazy* is published by Verve Poetry Press (2020). Together with her multi-instrumental live band, she leads *Genevieve Carver & The Unsung*: a cross-art form performance project celebrating unsung heroes and marginal voices. They released their first studio album *The Unsung* in 2017 and their latest show, *A Beautiful Way to be Crazy*, explores female experiences in the music industry. Genevieve is inspired by broken, imperfect things, music, and the sea. She also writes for theatre and television.

Twitter: @gevicarver

Grounding—Alicia Mietus

Alicia Mietus is a second-year Creative Writing MA student at Birkbeck University. She recently won the Queen Mary Wasafiri New Writing Prize 2019 for the fiction story *Third Person Female* and has read her work at MIRLive, the Mechanics Institute Review spoken word event. Current interests include the role of women, the immigrant experience, cultural and generational clashes, feminism and identity. She is working towards a short story collection and also has interests in screen and play writing.

Twitter: @MintAlicia

The Gestation Period of a Lemon—Holly Gammage

Since completing my MA in Creative and Critical Writing last September, I have been working as a Waterstones bookseller (and consequently spending all my wages on piles of glorious books). *The Gestation Period of a Lemon* is just one story in a surrealist, dreamlike collection I wrote for my dissertation. I also studied Fashion Journalism at Central Saint Martins for a year, before venturing to Winchester to pursue my love for writing fiction, via a BA in Creative Writing.   Since turning my attention to short fiction over the past four years, I have noticed a significant shift in my writing. More than anything, I want to continue to experiment with the form, and to see what strange surprises lay in wait. In the coming months, I will be taking time to polish my short stories, to write new material, and to devour as many books as possible in the process. I hope, sometime soon, to have finally read every book on my shelf. *Ulysses* will be my downfall, I know it.

Twitter: @holly_gammage

Birthday—Andrew Savage

By day I am a home tutor living in Dover, teaching maths, science and English to pupils who are unable for one reason or another to attend school, but by night (well, early to mid-morning actually) I am a writer.

I've been writing for many years now, especially poems (very short ones which I tweet!) and songs: mostly just for my own relaxation and pleasure. I've never had anything published before, except in a handful of particularly obscure small press magazines way back in the 1980s.

Three years ago I turned my pen to fiction, and finished writing a novel last year. It's a ghost story (of sorts) called *Redstone Cottage*. Writing short stories has given me a chance to experiment with things like narrative voice, different tenses, and character, all of which will be incredibly useful experience I feel when I get around to redrafting my novel.

Twitter: @FullMoonPoet

The Land of Cardboard—Enzo Kohara Franca

Born in Brazil to Japanese and Italian parents, Enzo moved alone to England at the age of eighteen to become a writer. After years hitch-hiking around Europe and the Middle East, he studied Photojournalism at the University of Arts London and documented conflicts in Eastern Ukraine and North Macedonia.

His fiction has been published by the Fortnightly Review (*Tradition*), the Tishman Review (*Other Americans*), What Now (*Liar's League*) and short-listed for the 2019 Tillie Olsen Award.

He has recently finished his first novel.

Twitter: @EkoharaFranca

Curious Tom—Peter Hankins

Peter spent many years pecking out a novel on his iPad while sitting with his elbows pressed together on commuter trains, travelling to and from his civil service job. He also had a long-running blog *Conscious Entities* about philosophy, the mind, and artificial intelligence, commended by academics but never likely to turn him into an internet influencer. Since retiring, he has focused on short stories, trying to build up his skills and obtain some much-needed encouragement. Happily, his stories have been shortlisted or placed in a number of competitions, including the Alpine Fellowship Prize, the Bridport short story competition, and the Hammond House International Writing Competition. He is now plotting to get that novel (about a quirky happy family trying to cope with the arrival of the Permissive Society in the East Midlands in 1968) back into motion.

Twitter: @peter_hankins

A Bell, a Step, a Cry—Alys Hobbs

Alys is a writer with a passion for all things dark and devilish. Born in Norfolk, she moved to Sheffield in 2009 to study Creative Writing at Sheffield Hallam university, and has stayed up North ever since. Alys began her career writing greetings cards for Hallmark, and now works as a copywriter across Yorkshire's creative scene. She lives in an ancient cottage in Derbyshire, where she spends most of her year planning Halloween parties and existing on a steady diet of ghost stories, crisp sandwiches and slow cat blinks. Alys has previously been published in literary journals such as *Popshot*, *The Ghastling Magazine* and the Kandisha Press *2020 Women of Horror* anthology.

Twitter: @hobzle

Unexpected—Alexandra Marie Bielby

Alexandra is a writer and textile artist. She has entered one other writing competition in the last couple years with a children's fairy tale. She has also had artwork displayed at the Sheffield Botanical Gardens *Art in the Gardens 2018* and *The Great Sheffield Art Show 2019*. She moved back to her mother's home city of Sheffield from Toronto sixteen years ago. In that time, she was a student at

Sheffield Hallam University, was diagnosed with a brain tumour, met her partner Simon and started going to a regular writing group. She is currently working on a young adult novel, set in a futuristic world that is living with the consequences of the environmental damage we have created.

Instagram: @lexible_84

The Judges

Emma Bolland

Emma is an artist and writer who works across literatures, translations, script and screenwriting, performance, and the moving image. They were the 2019 artist-writer in residence for the School of Arts and Humanities at the University of Sheffield, and are currently an Associate Lecturer for the BA, MA, and MFA Fine Art at Sheffield Hallam University. Their most recent monograph is *Over, In, and Under*, published by Dostoyevsky Wannabe in 2019.

Julianne Pachico

Julianne is the author of *The Lucky Ones* (2017) and *The Anthill* (which will be published in May 2020 in the UK, US, and Colombia). She grew up in Cali, Colombia, and lived there until she was eighteen. She has a PhD in creative writing from the University of East Anglia in England, where she is now a lecturer. Her story *Honey Bunny* appeared in *The New Yorker*, and two of her stories have been anthologized in *Best British Short Stories 2015*. In 2015 she was long-listed for the *Sunday Times* EFT Short Story Award and in 2017 she was short-listed for the *Sunday Times* Young Writer of the Year Award.

Niki Chang

Niki Chang is a literary agent at The Good Literary Agency. She represents writers of fiction and non-fiction and poets from under-represented backgrounds. She started her career at Aitken Alexander Associates before moving to TGLA. In 2019 she won the London Book Fair Trailblazer Award.

With huge thanks to:

David Oakley—for making it possible.

The Judges:
Julianne Pachico, Emma Bolland, Niki Chang

Panel Readers:
Denise Eaton, Joe Willis, Stephen Mellor, Liz Champion, David Oakley (again) and Letty Butler

The Kurious Press Team:
Lorna Partington Walsh (ideal-type.com),
Steven Kay (1889 Books Ltd),
Anne Grange (annegrangewriting.com),
Anna Caig (annacaigcomms.co.uk),
Mel Small (melsmall.com),
Stephen Mellor (Kurious Arts and stephenmellor.net)

Kurious?

This is the first publication from Kurious Press, a new independent publisher run by writers and editors from within the membership of Kurious Arts and Sheffield's creative community. Run by writers for writers, Kurious Press will provide a platform for new and innovative work from emerging and established writers.

If you have enjoyed the fruit of our collective efforts, it would be lovely if you could leave a review on Amazon, Goodreads, your blog or wherever. Many thanks.